Detective Donut
and the Wild Goose Chase

To George and our new friends for inviting us to the party and
supplying the donuts
—Bruce and Rosie

Detective Donut and the Wild Goose Chase
Copyright © 1997 by Bruce Whatley and Rosie Smith
Printed in the U.S.A. All rights reserved.

Library of Congress Cataloging-in-Publication Data
Whatley, Bruce.
   Detective Donut and the wild Goose chase / by Bruce Whatley and Rosie Smith.
     p.   cm.
   Summary: Detective Donut and his partner, Mouse, set out to find Professor Drake, the world-
famous archaeologist who has mysteriously disapppeared.
   ISBN 0-06-026604-X. —— ISBN 0-06-026607-4 (lib. bdg.)
   [1. Mystery and detective stories.]   I. Smith, Rosie, 1956–   II. Title.
PZ7.W5495De   1997   96-24505
[E]——dc20   CIP
                                                        AC

Typography by Tom Starace
1 2 3 4 5 6 7 8 9 10 ❖
First Edition

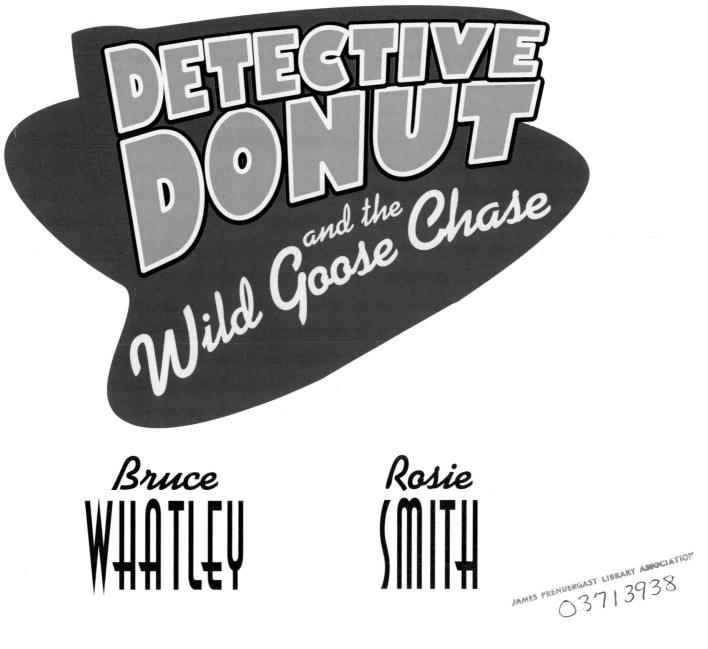

DETECTIVE DONUT
and the Wild Goose Chase

Bruce WHATLEY
Rosie SMITH

HarperCollins*Publishers*

I woke up with my head in my hands.
It had been a long night.
My last case had gotten the better of me.
Besides, it was my birthday, and nobody had remembered.
Worst of all, my partner had eaten the last donut.
Then came a knock at the door.
"Yeah," I said.

This strange bird walked through my door.
"Donut?" she asked.
"Yes, please," I said, "and a hot chocolate."
"Donut," she said again, "I need your help."
Then she told me she worked for Professor
Drake, the famous archaeologist.
"Professor Drake is missing!" said the bird.
"I need you to find him. He's got a statue
that he needs me to take to the museum."

Professor Drake and I were old friends.
I first met him at the museum.
That notorious thief, Goose, had stolen a priceless mummy, and the Professor had helped me track down Goose and put him behind bars.
Which reminded me, my mother owed me a birthday present.
Anyway, the Professor often traveled to far-off lands to search for ancient treasure.
He usually told me before he left, though.
Maybe this time he had forgotten.
He had also forgotten to tell me he had an assistant.

How could I say no?
I set out to look for my old friend.
On the way out, I picked up my mail.
A couple of bills, a postcard, and a strange-
looking package with a Maltese stamp.
I figured the package was a birthday present
from my mother.
Funny, I didn't know she was on vacation.
But right now I had more important things to
do than open my mail.
I was on a case, and I knew just how to begin.
I'd follow my nose.

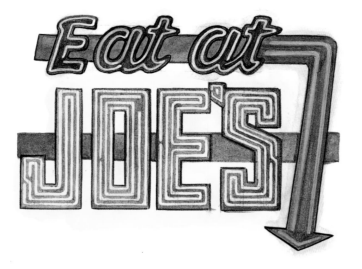

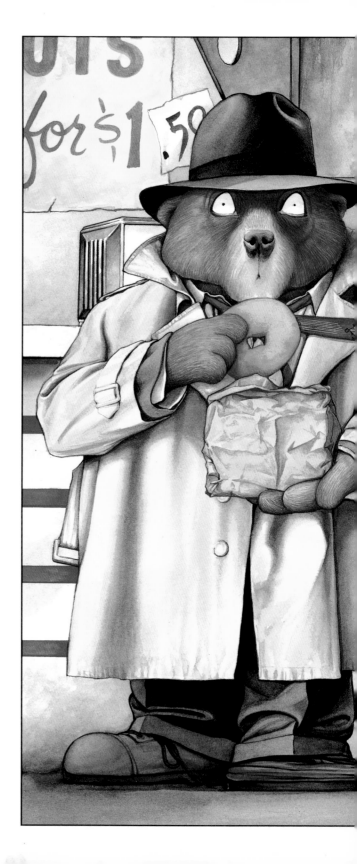

To Joe's Donuts.

Hey, I was still out of donuts!

Eating a donut or two always makes me think better.

It was after my third donut that I had my first big break.

Unfortunately, it was my big toe.

And I seemed to have lost my birthday present.

My mother usually knitted me a pair of socks
for my birthday.
I can always use a good pair of socks.
But why would anyone want my socks?
I must have been daydreaming.
One minute my package was gone.
The next minute it was back again.
I had to get my mind back on the job.
In this line of work, if you aren't careful,
you can end up with egg on your face.

It was time to head to the Professor's house
to check things out.
I got a surprise when I got there.
Someone had turned the place upside down.
I guess they were looking for something.
Something really valuable.
Something the Professor didn't want anyone
to find.
I realized the Professor could be in real danger!
And that's when the lights went out.

By the time the lights came back on,
someone had turned me upside down.
And my birthday present was gone.
Then I heard a noise coming from the alley
outside.
The thief was trying to make a break for it.
I took off after him. What did this guy want
with my birthday socks?

As I ran down the alley, I started to get mad.
Real mad.
I was supposed to be looking for the
Professor, but I was chasing my own birthday
present instead.
My socks would be too big for this guy
anyway.
And this dark alley was enough to give you
goose bumps.

The thief got away, but I found my package
in the trash.
I guess my socks were too big for him after all.
It had been a long day.
I needed a donut. So I headed for Joe's.
Turns out I wasn't the only one.
The Professor's assistant was right behind me,
looking a little worse for wear.
"Seen the Professor?" I asked.
"Over there!" she yelled.

"Where? Where?" I shouted as I looked over
my shoulder.
I couldn't see anyone.
When I turned back around, I couldn't see
my birthday present either.
This just wasn't my day.

Suddenly, there was a crash.
Next thing I knew, the Professor's assistant was flat as a pancake.
Then it hit me.
The Professor didn't have an assistant.
It was the notorious Goose himself, trying to make off with my socks.
"I've been framed!" shouted Goose.
"That's what they all say," I said.
I had caught him red-handed.
Meanwhile, my package had broken open on the floor, and there was no sign of my socks.
Just some dusty statue.
I couldn't figure out why Goose was trying to swipe my present, especially since it wasn't my socks.
But I didn't have time to worry about that now.
The Professor was still missing.
So I went back to my office
to think things over.

Dear Donut,
I am sending you
a very valuable statue
from Malta.
I know I can trust
you to take it to the
museum.
Goose has escaped
again and I'm afraid

POSTCARD

That's when I remembered my mail.
One of the bills was for the phone.
The postcard was from Professor Drake.
It said he knew Goose was on the loose and
was coming after him to steal the statue.
I quickly deduced that the package wasn't
from my mother after all.
The Professor had sent me the statue for
safekeeping while he hid out from Goose.
The postcard said the Professor would come
out of hiding after I had delivered the statue
safely to the museum.
The Professor would be so pleased to hear
how I single-handedly closed the case and
kept the statue safe.

And my mother had remembered my birthday after all.
While I was out, she had dropped off my birthday socks. They were red and a perfect fit.
She had also baked my favorite birthday cake. It had been another long day, and another case was closed.
Suddenly the lights went out.
The other bill was for the electricity.